The Distance of Mercy

A Novella

The Distance of Mercy

A Novella

by
Shelly Milliron Drancik

For Ethan, Mara, and Camille

Special gratitude to Kelly Simmons whose insight and encouragement kept me writing and rewriting. Thanks to Steven Rinehart, my MFA thesis advisor, for his perspective and guidance, and to the faculty and graduate students I had the benefit of working with at Queens University of Charlotte, especially Heather Marshall, Carla Damron, and Betty Joyce Nash.

Appreciation for my mom, my family, and my friends, Laura Haas and Christine Nolan, who have supported me in this process.

Thank you to the editors and team at Unsolicited Press for their work and dedication. I'm deeply grateful.

Nobody understands another's sorrow,
and nobody another's joy.

- Franz Schubert

You will never know the truth.

Seven years before I was born, a broadcast of Schubert's *Unfinished Symphony* played as my father watched hatred march into our city of Vienna. Hitler shared our blood, and many believed this was the reason not one shot was fired to keep the Germans away from our country. It was named the War of Flowers. My father scorned his countrymen who accepted serpent as savior. Even the Church was not safe from his contempt.

Each of my grandfathers were early members of the Nazi party. My mother's parents lived in a small town on the way to Salzburg. Their home, surrounded by rose gardens and enclosed by low limestone walls, served as a meeting place for high-ranking officials. My grandmother served selected meats and cheeses, *tortes,* coffee, and peppermint schnapps late into many nights, my mother told me.

I

My father's family lived in Salzburg, where Mozart was born. The day my father refused to play for Hitler's orchestra, his father disowned him, severed him from the family and its wealth. My grandfather instructed my father to keep the violin, declared it useless if not for the enjoyment of the Third Reich. The instrument, he told my father, would always serve as a reminder of how he had forsaken his heritage, forsaken true beauty, for Jews.

August 1967
Chicago

The girl ended up at my door. Well, Mrs. Forde told
me to expect her, said that some college student called
her about the job. I opened the door and there she was,
this girl. Didn't hint of a smile, looked kinda scared,
like maybe she never seen a Negro before. Or maybe it
was my size. I am an ample-sized woman.

"Hello," I said, my eyes scanning her.

She was tall enough, kind of boney looking, with
a pale face and dusty brown hair.

"Don't look much like one," I said. "Could use
more meat on them bones. Come in anyways."

She followed me inside with these hesitating
footsteps that made me wonder how she got the nerve
to come here in the first place.

"My name is Nicolette," she said.

"I know your name, child," I said. "Mrs. Forde
said you'd be here tonight." I looked at my wristwatch.
"A half-hour ago. She likes me to meet her applicants
before she hires them. I been with her for years." I put
out my hand and smiled. "I'm Tillie."

Nicolette looked at my hand as if it somehow
offended her. She finally took it but with this funny

little shake. Mrs. Forde told me she was foreign and I could tell she was strange from the start.

"I am late. I am sorry. I ride the—"

"—what's that accent you got?" I said. "Mrs. Forde didn't tell me where you was from."

"I am from Austria."

"Austria? Is that so?" I said. "You mean like *The Sound of Music* Austria?"

She nodded.

"Ain't that something now?"

I sure liked that movie with all them children singing songs in clothes cut from curtains. "That outfit you got on ain't made from a curtain, now is it?" I laughed, but she didn't seem to get my joke. "Okay then. You ever done this kind of work before? I hear you Germans are good cleaners."

"I am not German. I am Austrian—"

What's the difference, I wanted to tell her, but kept my mouth shut. "Well you know how to clean, right?" I wondered what Jimmy would of thought about me working with a German.

"Yes."

"What about England. Ever been there?" I said.

"No."

"That's where my husband was stationed. I'd like to know someone who been there, you know, tell me what it's like."

The girl looked all confused.

"You understanding me?" I said. "I don't need no communication problems. We got enough of 'em in this city as it is." I took a deep breath. "Here, have a seat." I gestured toward the couch for her to sit down. "My tongue is dry as dust. I need me a Tab before we get to talking. Want one?"

Nicolette's eyes pinched up looking confused again. She repeated the word.

"Tab?"

"A Tab," I said. A little louder than I should of. "Girl, you don't know what a Tab is?" I pretended to drink from an imaginary cup. "A pop."

"No," she said, still looking all confused. "Thank you."

"Be right back then." Right when I was leaving the room, I noticed her eyeing the glass bowl with my Starbursts on the coffee table. "Help yourself," I said. But she didn't move. I turned back and pointed speaking clear as I could. "The. Can-dy."

Nicolette lifted the glass lid and put it on the table like it was made of diamonds. She took one Starburst. Now who takes only one piece of candy?

"Go ahead," I said. "Take more than that."

From the corner of my eye, I seen her reaching for more. Couldn't see how this arrangement was going to work out. I should just get on the phone and tell Mrs. Forde to find me another worker. One from America.

When I came back into the room with my ice-cold bottle of Tab, Nicolette was on the couch, leaning over feeling the brown shag carpet. She quick pulled her

5

hand up. I didn't say nothing, didn't want to make her feel uncomfortable. For all I knew, maybe that's what people did in her country, you know, feel the floor. I needed to at least finish the interview, to be polite about it.

I lowered myself into a wooden chair and rested my elbows on its arms. Sure felt good to sit after the day I had. I preferred the couch but didn't want to crowd the poor thing. I said, "So why you here in Chicago?"

"I came to America to study the violin."

"The violin? Really?"

She said, "Yes."

"Then you better put some rubber gloves on those hands of yours. I only use heavy-duty cleaners." I looked at her hands. "You got yourself a husband?"

"No." Her cheeks bloomed pink. "I stay at the boarding house. Men are not allowed."

"Yeah, I suppose these days girls are all about waiting. Waiting so they can do their own thing first. Whatever that thing is." I gave her a quick wink. "By the time I was your age, I was married and settled down."

I got myself up out of the chair and walked over to the bookshelf and picked up a photo of James in his uniform. I walked it back over and showed it to Nicolette. "That's my Jimmy. Handsome, ain't he?" I waited for her to nod. "He got killed in Normandy."

She looked at the photo longer than I thought she would of.

6

"In the war?" she said.

I shot a look at her. How else on God's green planet would he get killed over there? I ignored her lack of common sense and walked the photo back to the bookshelf. I turned back around. "When Jimmy got back, we was going to have a baby."

Nicolette looked down at her hands.

I eased myself back into the chair. Took a long, cold drink.

"So what you doing half-across the planet from your family? Or did any of them come over here with you?"

"No."

She looked back over at the bookshelf. Then her eyes started glancing around the apartment, like she was staking out the place.

Nicolette said, "*Oma* gave me money."

"Oma? Who's that?"

"Grandmother. My grandmother."

"Well that sure was nice of her. Your parents still there?"

She said, "My mother died when I was ten."

"Oh, I'm sorry to hear that. Every girl needs her mama. I'm a grown woman, and I still need mine. How'd she die? Was it the cancer?"

The girl didn't seem to understand the question.

I said, "The cancer got my Aunt Lucille. A year ago last month. Lord, have mercy. Has it been that long? Took her in less than six months. Them doctors opened her up and seen a full nest of it in there. Closed her right back up. We buried her on the hottest day of July, our tears mixing with our sweat, all of it running down our faces." I stopped. She didn't appear interested in hearing about my Aunt Lucille, or maybe she wasn't understanding what I was saying to her.

I said, "Well, then, what about your father?"

"He is in Vienna."

Getting information from this girl was like sucking blood from a rock.

"Vienna? So that's the city you from. Well, that's good he still alive."

Nicolette paused. "Yes."

Nothing more from her. Okay then.

So I said, "You got any brothers and sisters?"

"No."

"Not a one?" I said, a tone of disbelief shooting through my question. I smiled, but this girl didn't seem capable of returning one.

"Well, how'd you like the airplane ride?"

A strange look passed over her face. She made a quick gesture with her hands, almost made me laugh out loud.

"You mean you threw up?"

"Yes."

Good Lord. This girl required too many charades to communicate.

8

Then her eyes fixed back toward the bookshelf. Either at the wall of photos or at my collection of panda bears sitting on the shelves.

"What are you looking at, my nieces and nephews or them pandas?" I said. "See all them children. They gave me all them pandas. I seen this program once on PBS about them black and white bears over there in China. How they eat that plant that grows two foot every day. You know what I'm talking about? I must of mentioned that I liked them because now every birthday, every Christmas, every single time I unwrap a present, one of them bears be staring up at me." I laughed. "Now what's a grown woman in her forties supposed to do with all them toys?"

I took a drink. Nicolette started to rub her fingers with her thumb.

The phone rang. Just in time because this conversation was wearing me out more than the two apartments I cleaned today.

"Excuse me." I headed over to the phone and picked up the receiver.

"Hello?" I looked over at Nicolette. She was unwrapping another piece of candy and hurried to stick it in her mouth. "Yeah, she here." I paused. "Yeah. Well, not so sure." But I knew a few sentences into our conversation that Mrs. Forde was going to give this girl a chance. "Okay then. Okay, yes, on Tuesday. Bye." Anyways I didn't have time to sit through no more of these interviews. They cut into my evening tv shows.

9

I sat back down. "Now I really don't have time for all this chatting. Back to what brought you here. Mrs. Forde will pay you a dollar and fifty cent an hour. If you work hard, can be *on time,* and don't mind getting bleach on them shoes of yours, you can work with me. You hear me?"

Nicolette nodded. "Yes, I can hear you."

I tilted my head to the side. "No, I mean," I said speaking in slow syllables, "do you understand what I am saying to you?"

"Yes." She smiled a little. That was a first.

"Good," I said. "Hand me my purse over there."

Nicolette didn't move.

"My purse." I pointed to the side of the couch. She picked it up and handed it to me. I took out my little notebook that I like to carry with me and tore off a page, wrote down the address where'd we meet along with the time underlined and handed it to her.

I said, "Now that we got everything settled, I can get on with my evening. Lucy's coming on at 7:00. You like to watch her?"

Nicolette didn't respond, only stared at me.

"Okay then," I said, standing back up. "See you next Tuesday."

"Yes," she said.

I walked her to the door. "Have a nice night." I said. "Bye."

And then she left.

Nicolette was something all right. Always swimming in her thoughts. My grandmother used to say you could tell a lot about a person without them speaking a word, but I couldn't tell a thing about this one. Most days she was so lost in her own world, I wanted to take and shake her into this one.

On Tuesday and Thursday mornings, the days Nicolette worked with me, we met early outside a diner. Being new to the city, she didn't know whether to take the bus or the L to our jobs, and I needed to make sure she got there.

To my surprise, she never was late meeting me again. I heard that some foreigners be late on their own wedding day. All I know is they wouldn't be working with me.

Today, we was cleaning at Ray's. I have the key to some of my regulars' apartments so when I was opening the door, I seen him passed out on the couch. Most mornings this was how I found him.

Nicolette stared at him. "He is dead?" she said.

"Poke him." I laughed. "He ain't any more dead than me. He just hungover."

She stood as still as stone.

"Girl, I rather he be passed out like this instead of following me around like that lady over there on Kenmore last week." I picked up a handful of Ray's empty beer cans. "Swishing after me in her housedress, following me to every last room. Hanging on to her Hollywood magazine like it was the Bible. What'd she think? I was gonna slip something of hers in my pocket. I wanted to tell her, now, lady, what would I do with an orange ceramic owl or a tiny green glass basket that only fit ten jellybean? I wanted to tell her, don't you worry, I got my own knickknacks. I got my pandas." I paused and nodded toward Ray. "He just had too much fun last night."

Nicolette kept looking at him instead of getting to her work.

"If he bothering you, go on and vacuum in the bedroom."

She quick went down the hall.

"Vacuum's in the hall closet," I called after her.

After I took care of his beer cans and emptied the ashtray full of them nasty butts, I carried my things to the bedroom. Nicolette was dusting, vaguely.

I said, "Why ain't you vacuuming like I told you?"

"I do not want to wake him."

"Why not? We got a job to do. It ain't my problem he had too much to drink last night." I said, looking closely at her, "And how about you? What'd you do last night?"

Without hesitating, she said, "I walked to the cemetery."

"The cemetery?" I said. "Good Lord, someone you know die already?"

"No," she said.

"Well, why'd you go there?"

"I played my violin."

"In the cemetery?"

"Yes."

12

"You mean to tell me that you walked to the graveyard then you had the nerve to play your violin to a dead person, a dead person you don't even know?" This girl was too much.

"Yes."

"You just stood there by someone's gravesite and played your instrument?"

"In Vienna, I play at my mother's gravesite."

"Well that's good and sweet for your mama, but you need to know—in this country—that's grounds for getting picked up by the police and taken to the ward for coo-coo's."

Nicolette started dusting the nightstand, her back to me.

I said, "Did I tell you my sisters are dying to meet you?"

They would eat up the story about the cemetery.

"Why do they want to meet me?" she said.

"I tell them a lot about you."

Nicolette stopped dusting and turned around. "Why?"

"I don't know," I said. "You just different." Blanche and Jackie ain't never met no violin player from Austria; I went on. "Their names are Blanche and Jackie, and Blanche was the one of us always getting into mischief as a child. Don't know how many times my mama or grandmother had to use a switch on her." Nicolette was watching the words come out of my mouth. I said, "Here, help me strip the bed." I yanked at the corner. "Anyways, the saliva in that girl's mouth was pure acid, the way she spoke to Mama. Hand me that pillow. And Jackie, the mild child, all she ever wanted to do was be grown, get married and have babies. Well she had them babies but skipped the married part. Now her babies are having babies." I threw the sheets in a bundle on the floor. "Know what I'm saying?"

I couldn't tell if she could or couldn't. I started on the dresser mirror and she went back to dusting. I told her that Blanche had a good federal job for some twenty years now, it was the place that printed my check for Jimmy, that's why she only had time for two kids. But her husband, that man was really was her third child. Only worked side jobs, yet every time I seen him he got on a new shirt from Fields, always some pastel color, like he trying to look like some dyed Easter egg.

I said, "Blanche could of done better than him but I got tired of telling her what she already knew."

Nicolette looked like she was going to ask a question but didn't.

"Listen," I said. "Next time we have a family gathering, I'll bring you along. You can meet the whole family but don't say I didn't warn you. People be dropping in throughout the day fixing their plates while me and my sisters trying to keep our brother, Thomas, away from the bottle."

Nicolette looked at me with those murky grey eyes of hers. She said, "The family is yours."

I stood there for a second. What did she mean by that? "Of course, my family is mine. One that can get on my last nerve." I looked at my watch. "Get vacuuming now. Time for Ray to get his day going."

Nicolette nodded and went to plug in the cord.

~~~

I was born in Vienna at the end of the Second World War, in the midst of a cold spring following a bitter winter, as Austria's flag of red and white stripes taunted Hitler's holding army. My mother told me I was born at dusk, as bombs shattered the sky into colors recognized alone by God.

The midwife called my father from the living room where he stood by the rattling windows of our flat. Papa named me Nicolette, telling Mama it meant victory of the people. Other Viennese waited in cellars or bomb shelters, waiting for the Americans or the Russians, any force that would end Hitler's rule.

A week after my birth, the Red Army entered Vienna.

My country was soon divided into four zones controlled by America, England, France, and the Soviet Union. My family lived in a flat in *Wieden*, the fourth district of Vienna, one controlled by the Russians.

When I was old enough, every Sunday afternoon after we walked home from Mass at *Karlskirche*, Papa sat back in his chair and said, "Nicolette, the violin."

Tired from the long liturgy and the priest's endless words, I wanted to take my doll to Anya's next door where sounds from siblings chasing one another shook their flat. Or I wanted to sit on my bedroom floor and let my thoughts float like the painted clouds and cherubs on the dome of *Karlskirche.*

I walked past pages of scores piled and scattered on the floor to the wooden trunk where the violin was kept in its case and carried it toward Papa, his left hand resting on his knee, red and useless.

Though I never heard Papa play the violin, I saw the music in his eyes, heard it in the taps of his foot.

He asked, "Did you practice every day this week?"

"Yes, Papa, every day. Almost."

"Almost?"

I glanced at Mama preparing our evening meal in the kitchen, her beauty apparent in the afternoon light.

She said to him, "I let Nicolette miss practice on Friday. She looked so tired after her school week." Her eyes met mine, directing me to pay attention to Papa.

After I tightened the strings like Papa had instructed me, I began my scales. When I moved the bow across the strings, releasing each note, he said, "Yes! Good! Continue."

Within a short time, the violin, heavy and awkward on my thin shoulder, and the chin rest that made my chin itch, caused me to complain and my notes to sound like screeches against the air.

He said, "Now play the Mozart I assigned you."

"Papa, I don't play that one well."

"Yet," he said, "he wrote it at a younger age than you?"

"Please, Papa, choose an easier one." I hesitated. "Anya plays with her doll on Sundays."

"Easier is not acceptable. The violin will save you someday, Nicolette, not a doll."

I glanced at his hand, then continued to play.

When I finished, I knew by Papa's expression that I'd never be the violinist he wanted me to be. I loosened the strings and placed the violin in its case and watched Papa walk toward Mama standing by the kitchen sink. He wrapped his arm around her waist and kissed the bend of her neck. She leaned back into him. The three of us made our family, but in such moments, I felt as if there were only two.

Every week Mama took me on processions to the shrines in Vienna. Led by a Franciscan priest, the Holy Rosary Crusade prayed for the withdrawal of the Soviet Union from our country. A tithe of Austrians, a tenth of the population, wrapped rosary beads around hands and wrists, reciting prayer after prayer, week after week, year after year. Through rain, through snow, through heat that pasted my dress to my skin, I walked alongside my mother.

When Saint Stephen's Cathedral reopened to the people, the cathedral's bells chimed, their ringing carried by restless spring air. Crowds circled the cathedral on the cobblestoned square waiting for the doors to open. I held Mama's hand, feeling the bells' vibrations inside my chest, wondering why one tower stretched higher than the other. Mama wiped away tears.

An old man with white whiskers poking from his chin bent down toward me. I had never met my grandparents, had never been around anyone that old and quickly backed away from him, afraid that his whiskers would scratch my cheek.

He said, "Guess, child, how many bells are inside?"

I did not answer him, only looked at Mama. The old man stood upright and said, "Twenty-two." He smiled at me. "Without the *Pummerin*, but she'll return soon. The largest bell in Austria."

Mama took my hand and walked me closer to the entrance. Our fingers touched its cold limestone wall. She directed my fingers to feel the engraved numerals, 05, *Osterreich*, told me it was a secret symbol of Austria's resistance. The man with whiskers moved toward us again.

He said, "Did your parents tell you the story of the *Pummerin*?"

I looked at him but did not respond.

"Well, did they?" he said.

"No, sir." I looked at Mama.

"Don't know why parents don't tell their children our history." He pointed to the higher tower. "Kept up there until it crashed to the floor during the war. Made from Turkish cannons. Ruined by the Allies."

The old man looked directly at Mama.

Mama said, "My daughter was born just before we were liberated by the Allies. There is nothing more we need to tell her."

"My son was killed. Fought against the *Führer*. That's why I'm here. To see if I can forgive him."

Mama said, "Excuse us, sir," as she tried to steer us away from him.

The old man continued, "It was the Allies who burned this cathedral."

Mama turned around and said, "It was the war."

"Left us with the Russians, worse than any German," he said. "Breaking into wine cellars, drinking our wine. Taking our women because their skin is smoother than the grainy-skinned wives they left behind. You heard the screams. Or maybe your good husband knew not to let you out of your flat at night?"

"Come, Nicolette." She pulled my hand harder but the crowd prevented us from moving.

"You can stop praying the rosary. The Russians will never leave."

At last there was movement in the crowd and we were able to enter the cathedral through the massive door.

Inside, the ceiling soared above us and I felt like a miniature doll. Bronze and white tiles gleamed beneath us. The high altar seemed to float in the distance. People flocked to light candles to the right. Mama kept me close to her. As we walked past the statues of saints on columns, I felt their stone eyes watching me.

Mama walked me past a pulpit with carved toads and salamanders and a barking dog.

"Mama, look! Look at that dog. They don't let animals inside churches. Why is he barking?"

"Put your finger down. I'm sure there's a reason. Maybe he's barking at the devil. Come this way."

"But why would a toad and salamander chase one another in a church?"

"I don't know. They're symbols. Ask your father."

"Papa doesn't like it when I ask questions."

"He doesn't mind if you ask the right ones." She pulled on my hand for me to follow her. "Come with me, Nicolette. I want to show you something."

Mama and I approached the left chapel in the choir that displayed a gilded, open-winged wooden altarpiece of the Virgin Mary holding her infant son.

Mama said, "Mary is between Saint Catherine and Saint Barbara, the one with the tower in her hands."

The painted wooden faces of the Virgin Mary and Saint Catherine were serene, joyful, but it was the eyes of Saint Barbara which spoke to me.

"A tower?" I said. "It looks like a toy."

"It's not a toy, Nicolette. Her father kept her in a stone tower when she told him she wanted to become a Christian. He sent her teachers in philosophy and poetry. He wanted her to remain a pagan like him."

"What happened to her?"

"She became a Christian and died for her faith."

"Will you tell me her story at bedtime?"

21

Mama said, "No, I want to tell you about Saint Catherine."

"But I want to hear about Saint Barbara. Who killed her?"

Mama paused. "That's not important."

I said, "Was she burned up like Joan of Arc?"

"Nicolette Stolicz! Never make light of a saint's death. It's not how she died. It's why she died."

"Did God want her to die?"

"No," Mama said then looked toward the altar. She put her arm around my shoulder. "But He wants us to have the same faith. Saint Joan was on a military crusade to save her country. We're on a spiritual one to save ours. That's why we need to keep praying."

"So the soldiers leave?"

"Yes. So we have our freedom. Come now. I need to light a candle for my father before we leave."

"Papa won't like that."

"Yes, I know. But he was my father."

We started to walk back toward the entrance. I glanced around.

I said, "I don't want to see that old man with the whiskers again. He smelled."

"Now, Nicolette, you must not say that, even if he is an old swine."

~~~

I asked Nicolette to meet me for breakfast on a Tuesday morning inside the diner and told her that she needed to be there a half hour earlier than normal. It was my birthday, but I didn't want her to know and make a fuss about it. If you have to work on the day you was born, you should at least have someone else cook breakfast for you.

When she saw me, she gave me the once over. I'm used to people outside of my neighborhood looking at me like that, scanning their eyes all up and down me. Today I had on my white overalls and red t-shirt and a bandana around my neck. Overalls were good for their pockets during a cleaning job; then after, I'd throw them in a bucket of bleach and let the bleach do all the scrubbing.

Nicolette said hello.

"Grab that table by the window," I said. "Hurry."

I followed behind her.

Nicolette slid into the booth first. Across from her, I shifted my body along the red vinyl seat of the booth and then rested my forearms on the table. She started making circles with her fingers on the Formica table. What was with this girl and her feeling things?

The waitress came over looking like she could of used another half-night's sleep. She said, "You need to *wait* to be seated."

I said, "Oh, sorry, first time inside here. We'd like to see some menus please."

The waitress plucked them from under her arm and dropped them on the table. They almost slipped onto the floor, but I grabbed them before they fell.

I looked at her, smiled, and said, "Thank you."

The waitress turned away, and I started reading the menu. I glanced up and saw Nicolette staring at people around the diner. Then she had the nerve to ask me why people were looking at us.

"Girl, if you stop gaping at them, they'll stop gaping at us. Don't mind them. Just look at that menu in front of you. I'm hungry."

But Nicolette kept looking around so I said, "Remember that greystone house we stopped cleaning a couple of weeks ago? Mrs. Forde got a call from the woman saying she didn't feel *comfortable* with a colored person—like I'm from some crayon box— in her house after all. No matter that I was cleaning her soiled toilets."

Nicolette looked down at her menu. I kept explaining.

"So Mrs. Forde told this woman that was fine since she herself didn't feel *comfortable* taking money from a woman of *her* kind. But these people in here are just curious." I took a breath. "Know what you want?"

But she was reading the menu so slow it was like watching honey drip off of a spoon. When the waitress finally came back to take our order, Nicolette ordered ham, toast, and coffee. I ordered eggs over easy, toast, extra bacon and a Tab. Then I seen Nicolette looking around the place again.

She said, "This is different than *kaffehaus* in Vienna."

"Well," I said, "what do you expect? You in America." I noticed my tone had a slap to it, so I toned it down. "Just so you know. I'm paying." Then I let it slip. "It's my birthday."

"Yes," Nicolette said, but didn't follow-up with even a happy birthday. Maybe over there they don't celebrate birthdays.

"How about this weekend you come with me to Mama's? She's cooking a feast. Everyone will be there for my birthday."

Nicolette said, "No, thank you."

"Well, why not?" I said. "Beats hanging out in cemeteries." My patience was starting to wear thin with her.

The waitress returned with Nicolette's coffee cup and my Tab.

I was about to ask for a glass of ice, but the waitress had already left.

Nicolette opened five creamers and poured them in her cup. I shook my head. Then I started up a conversation, with me asking her questions about her boarding house and classes, and she giving me her half-answers, telling me next to nothing.

When the waitress set our food in front of us, Nicolette asked me, "Why is bread in America so narrow?"

"What do you mean?"

"In Vienna, bread is thick, not narrow." Narrow? I never thought of bread being narrow. And where did she learn that word?

I said, "So it can fit in a toaster." I started on my breakfast.

When I seen she wasn't touching her slice of ham, it was just sitting there on her plate, I asked, "You going to eat that?"

"The meat is wet."

"Wet? That ain't wet, just a coating of oil. If you don't want it, give it here." I stabbed it with my fork and brought it to my plate. "If I ever left a piece of meat like that on my plate when I was a child, my mama would've hollered until I ate the thing."

She looked straight at me and God only knows what thoughts were running through her foreign little head.

I said, "Okay then, tell me, what was your mama like?"

Nicolette looked out the window.

"She was beautiful."

"And? What else?"

Still looking out the window, she said, "I do not remember."

The poor thing. Something told me not to push. "What about your father?"

"He played the violin."

"Oh, that how you learned to play?"

Like she didn't hear my last question, Nicolette said, "He loved my mother."

"Well, that's nice. Mine got up and left us for a woman down the street with no kids. He never did come home, and I never did forgive him even though the good book says I need to. My book says there ain't no way." I took a drink and set my bottle down with a little too much force. "So was he any good at the violin?"

"Yes." Then she looked out the window again. "Until the Germans shot his hand."

I needed a second to respond. "Shot his hand? With a gun?"

Nicolette looked back at me. "Yes."

"Dear Lord. Why?"

"Papa refused to play in Hitler's orchestra."

"Sweet Jesus. So they shot his hand?"

"Yes. He never talked about it." Nicolette hesitated but then went on. "Papa knew a farmer who refused to serve in the Nazi army. He was beheaded."

This was way too much, way too early in the morning. Still my mouth got ahead of me and I couldn't help asking, "Like John the Baptist?"

Nicolette paused. "Yes," she said.

"He's a hero then, like my Jimmy."

Nicolette looked down at her plate and started moving her food around with her fork.

"Tell me something else about him."

Nicolette looked up at me and said, "He composes, like Schubert."

"Schubert? Who's Schubert?"

"A famous composer." Now she looked at me like I was the crazy one.

I asked, "Oh, like Beethoven?"

"Yes, like Beethoven." Then the girl actually smiled and her whole face shifted. To my surprise, she continued as if talking about dead composers was normal conversation for me.

"He is devoted to Schubert. That is how he found my mother."

I took the last drink of Tab. Not sure why, but I liked hearing about her family.

She continued. "When he was a new student at University, he walked down a corridor and heard a voice that made him stop. Mama sang "*Gretchen am Spinnrade.*" He waited for her outside the door with his back against the wall. He said that he felt like he was holding back the waters of the ocean itself." She looked out the window.

That wasn't how my parents met. They met on the street.

"So your mother was a singer?"

Nicolette looked back at me like I asked the wrong question.

She said, "She never sang, even when I asked her. Instead, at bedtime, she told me stories of the saints."

I said, "Oh. My mama sang to me at bedtime. Almost every night."

Nicolette looked like she was going back in that dark tunnel of hers. I thought she was going to cry, and I didn't do good with crying unless somebody died or was born. And anyways, it was my birthday. I looked at my watch. "We better get going. This lady is what we call in America a fusspot." I reached for my wallet inside my purse. "But wait till you see the inside of her house. Under her highfalutin skin, she ain't nothing but a slob."

~~~

Papa never told me stories of the saints when I was a girl; he told me stories about composers. His favorites were Haydn, Mozart, and Schubert. He told me about their early deaths and incomplete lives. He told me about Alma Rosé and her father, Arnold Rosé, but never spoke about Gustav Mahler, Alma's uncle.

Before Hitler's annexation of Austria, Alma and her parents lived in the fourth district, like my family, until her father became the concertmaster at the Vienna Philharmonic. Herr Rosé handed down his love of the violin to Alma, his only child. I asked Papa once if we lived in the same flat that the Rosé family had lived in, but he shook his head and laughed. Without reason, I envied hearing about Alma, imagining her bedroom when she was a girl filled with porcelain dolls with rose-colored cheeks and lace clothing with tiny buttons.

He told me Alma was married briefly to a Czech violinist then returned to Nazi occupied Vienna to care for her ill mother until she died; because of their Jewish roots, she and her father fled to England.

When Alma was not able to earn enough money to support them, she travelled to Holland to give concerts, always sending the money home to her father. Alma was soon captured when Hitler invaded Holland

and sent to Auschwitz-Birkenau. There, she was recognized and given a violin. They moved her to the Music Block to lead an orchestra of women with slight musical training and very few instruments. Alma's orchestra was forced to play for the prisoners walking into the fields at dawn, and again when they returned to the barracks at night, ravaged and weak.

"It was known in the camp," Papa told me many times, "if Alma selected a woman for her orchestra, the woman's life had been saved."

Alma died in spring the year before I was born. Officials at Auschwitz-Birkenau said that she died from tainted food from a can. Her body was displayed, her musicians allowed a few moments to pay their final respects; this, Papa told me, in a camp built to decimate humans.

Papa admired Alma for the orchestra she led, her drive for musical perfection, and the lives she saved, but I remember Alma for her loyalty as a daughter. If she had been freed, Alma would have returned at once to her waiting father in London.

In late November, alpine winds brought wet snow to our city. Mama promised me at breakfast that when I returned home from school, she would teach me how to prepare dumplings for our evening soup with the white flour she had received from Fräulein Elstein. Somehow Fräulein Elstein was able to acquire ingredients not found on the shelves of the greengrocers; once I saw her speaking with a Russian soldier down a narrow street close to her flat. The soldier's hands gestured rapidly while he spoke to her before he slipped something in her paper bag.

The school day seemed longer than usual as I sat in my stiff chair at the back of the classroom, my thoughts wandering toward the afternoon when Mama and I would work the flour into fresh dough.

After school, too impatient to wait for Anya, I ran home, the snow falling like cold kisses on my face. When I opened the door to our flat, I called out for Mama. From the bedroom, a Russian soldier strode toward me. He bent down to me, his breath bitter as if he had swallowed mothballs. I could not see my mother, only the red, five-pointed star that branded his uniform. When the soldier's fingers came close to my face, my throat refused to release its air. I stared at my shoes, watching the melted snow run down the black leather. I closed my eyes and prayed in silence. *Hail Mary, full of Grace, the Lord is with you. Blessed are you among women, and blessed is the fruit of thy womb, Jesus*—The soldier said something in Russian, and then I heard my mother's voice, felt her grip my arm. I opened my eyes. My mother and the soldier exchanged Russian words that sounded like bullets within the walls of our quiet flat.

The soldier grabbed my mother's arm.

"Nicolette," my mother said. "Go next door."

My mother stood next to the soldier, her eyes like blue glass. The soldier drew Mama toward the bedroom. My head shook. My eyes blurred. I wanted to run and scream at the soldier. I wanted to scratch and tear at him. But my mother said "Go," and closed the bedroom door.

I ran from the building through snow that came down like thick white rain.

When I reached Saint Stephen's Cathedral, I went inside, water dripping from me onto the tile floor. Scattered people knelt in the pews. I stood alone in the back of the church for a long time, not knowing what to do.

~~~

Nicolette and me was getting on the L late in the afternoon and found two seats toward the middle. It was one of those warm late September days when the air wraps around your skin and makes you feel like you in God's hands.

As soon as I sat my tired bones down on the seat, Nicolette started gawking at everyone as usual, looking at them like we was at the zoo. Her country must lack variety of people.

A group of white girls, maybe a little younger than Nicolette, got on. Across the aisle from us, they was all giggling and having a good time over nothing. Their sweet sticky perfume almost made me sneeze. Don't know why their mamas don't teach them how to braid that hair to get it out of their faces. I noticed Nicolette watching these girls closely then touching her own hair all pulled back in a bun. And them shirts on these girls; they was these thin cotton shirts showing the world they were wearing no bras under them shirts. Lord have mercy. I wanted to tell them that showing your nipples through a t-shirt wasn't going to make the world a better place for females. The only thing it'd do was make men's eyeballs look at nothing but them nipples. I nudged Nicolette. We both needed to look elsewhere.

34

"I'm just curious," I asked Nicolette, trying to come up with a subject. "Since you getting a degree for that violin, how long do you practice every day?"

She looked at me. Today her eyes looked as murky as a pond.

"Six hours."

I let out a gasp. "You mean to tell me that you spend six hours, every day, practicing the violin? Six hours on one instrument, one thing?"

"Yes."

"How can you do that?"

"It keeps me in America."

With that girl, it was like I'd be asking her one question, and she be turning around giving me an answer to another one. I could feel my impatience rising again. I took a calming breath and said, "You must like it, seeing you have to spend that much time with it."

"No," she said, "I wanted to play the piano, but my father did not allow me."

"Well, I wanted to be a ballerina, but that didn't happen either." I took another calming breath. "I'd like to hear you play."

"No," Nicolette said. "I am not as good as the other students. I write Papa and tell him the compositions I learn. He writes me and tells me it is not good enough. He tells me he needs me. He tells me to come home."

"Already? You just got here."

She gave me one of her looks and said, "The doctors give him medicine for his mind."

"Oh, I see. I had an uncle like that. We had to take him to a special place downstate. Well why can't you go home for a visit? Maybe for Christmas?"

She said, "If I go home, they will not let me return."

"What do you mean? Who's they?"

Nicolette didn't respond. She turned her head away from me and started staring at them girls again.

~~~

Every week, the Russian soldier rapped on our door. The other soldiers in our district wore bland faces, one melting into another. His face, this Russian soldier, I knew apart from the others; his face was yellowed with a bulbous nose, lined with hair the color of mud. He always brought a gift for me, an item I was seldom allowed: a small jar of raspberry preserves, a piece of marzipan shaped like an apple just plucked from a tree, a blood orange with a fragrance that stayed on my fingers long after I had eaten it. I wanted to refuse each gift, but I took what he offered me, his forearm lined with wristwatches, before I left for Anya's flat.

Many days when I returned home for dinner, Papa was not home. If he had stopped at a *beisl,* I would not see him for the rest of the night. But he would always appear the next morning, sitting at our wooden table with a cup of black coffee, an empty liquor glass, and a cigarette burning in the ashtray. The nights when Papa came home, I wanted to tell him about the soldier, but the words stayed buried inside me. At our dinner table, I watched Mama, waiting for a sign to cross her face that would signal me to tell Papa about the soldier. The sign from her never appeared, and I learned to become part of my mother's secret.

An afternoon when I returned home from school, I heard Mama cry through the black wood of their bedroom door. When she came out of the bedroom, loose strands of hair hid her face. A knock brushed the front door. I waited for the soldier to push through, bringing his odor of tobacco and brandy and his small gift for me. In his place, a woman wrapped in grey woolen clothes filled the doorway.

"Come in please," my mother told her. "I expected you at noon. My daughter is home now." Mama turned to me. "Nicolette, go practice now."

When I passed the grey woman, she smelled of cloth left out in the rain.

"Yes, I see her," the woman said. "I suppose it is now close to *jause*."

In the corner of the living room, two splintered chairs sat under the window, the oak trunk between them. I pulled the violin from its case.

My mother asked the grey woman if she would like coffee.

The grey woman said, "Yes, and cake. Do you have cake?"

"No, I'm sorry. We don't but I will—"

"—Never mind with the coffee then."

Then the grey woman said, "And how do you feel?" placing her hand low on my mother's stomach. "You don't look good."

Mama's voice remained low. "May I come to you this week?" she said. "How many schillings?"

"Do you bleed?"

38

"No," my mother said.

"Are you certain…" the grey woman heaved, her round body consumed by her breath, "this is what you do?"

"How many schillings?" Mama said.

The grey woman said, "I tell you after."

Mama woke me early the next morning and gave me only a *kipferl* to eat. I tore a small piece off and swallowed the sour, dry bread. Mama then walked me to Fräulein Elstein's flat.

Fräulein Elstein had no children, no husband, only sewing to keep her hands occupied. The hunger gnawed at my stomach as we walked the four blocks in the early damp air.

When my mother prepared to leave, she placed her hands on my cheeks and spoke in a whisper, "*Meine Liebe.*" She kissed my forehead. "Now mind Fräulein Elstein. Come back here after school." Upset that I could not return home alone after school, I said no, using a tone of voice I had never used before with Mama.

"I will see you here after school," she said. The pain I caused her was apparent on her face. Mama turned to reach for the doorknob. As soon as the door closed behind her, I wished that I had said I was sorry to her.

When I returned to Fräulein Elstein's in the afternoon, she fed me a sandwich of cold sausage. She then pulled out her sewing basket, handed me a spool of thread, a needle, and a piece of yellow fabric. Fräulein Elstein sat in her burgundy, wing-backed chair. I tried to work with the thread, but my fingers were not used to thread so thin.

After a long while, Fräulein Elstein said, "When your father played in the orchestra, his friends would come not only to hear him play, but to see your mother." She looked out the window, yet her fingers continued to move. "They were so naïve." Her fingers became motionless. "I tried to warn your father. Look at what her beauty has cost them." She lifted the cloth and checked her stitch.

I wanted to ask her what she meant, but concentrated on untangling the knot I had made in the thread.

"I told your father," she said, "a long time ago." She looked at me, shook her head. "Give me the thread, Nicolette," she said taking it from me. "You are slow to learn."

When Mama arrived at the flat, she looked feverish. Fräulein Elstein made coffee for *jause*. No one besides me took a piece of the cake baked with fresh ginger.

I helped Fräulein Elstein clear the table while Mama sat. She did not seem interested in hearing about my school day. The three of us walked to our flat, Mama's slow, shuffled steps making us get caught in the rain. Close to home, I reached down to put a wet stone in my pocket.

Fräulein Elstein said, "Drop that, Nicolette. Come along. We don't need debris inside."

Mama looked at her but said nothing.

Inside, our flat was dark and empty. I felt Mama flinch when I touched her sleeve; her eyes looked beyond me. Fräulein Elstein put my mother to bed and told me to start the water for potatoes. I heard nothing but my own footsteps on the wooden floors. No one came to help me light the stove. I filled the pot and waited for the water to boil. My hands scrubbed the potatoes. When the bubbles appeared and exploded into the skim of the water, I dropped the potatoes in one by one.

Mama and Fräulein Elstein did not come out to eat dinner. Papa did not return home. I left two plates of potatoes and thick slices of dark *landbrot* at the door of the bedroom. With my ear to the door, I listened but there was only silence. I practiced my violin twice as long as was required. At bedtime, I changed into my nightdress and then slowly cracked my parents' bedroom door. A smell of dampness from the window left open filled the room. I heard the faint taps of Mama's rosary beads. Fräulein Elstein sat in the corner chair with her sewing in her lap, her fingers pulling the needle through the fabric in perfect rhythm. Through the dim light I saw Mama's body curled on the bed with only a thin linen to protect her from the chilled air. Without looking up, Fräulein Elstein said, "Your mother is very ill. Let her rest."

I said, "Goodnight, Mama." Before I closed the door, I thought I heard Mama whisper the words, my child.

Later in the night I heard Papa return home. I got out of bed and opened my door. Father Vogl was with Papa carrying a small jar of consecrated oil and a prayer book in his hands. He followed Papa into the bedroom, closing the door behind them. I went to the door and sat against the wall. When Father Vogl came out of the bedroom, he saw me and crouched beside me, blessed me, and crossed himself.

Papa came out of the bedroom and walked Father Vogl to the door. I followed them.

Father Vogl said, "You will call Paulina's family?"

"It's too late," Papa said.

His words covered my head like a heavy cloak.

The priest said, "Mercy is never too late."

But Papa had turned away and was walking back toward the bedroom. Father Vogl placed his hand on my shoulder and then left.

~~~

Somehow the calendar got flipped all the way to December, and for three days in the middle of the month, the sky did nothing except let out snow, heavy and wet. It snowed so much that it got us out of work on Tuesday. I didn't like to miss work and the wages that came with it, but when she called, Mrs. Forde said she'd still pay us. An early Christmas present. Don't know why God don't churn out more people like her.

Mrs. Forde asked me if Friday we could do a job, a favor for a friend of hers. This friend's daughter was on bedrest and her normal cleaning lady got snowed in out East. When Mrs. Forde told me that she was throwing a birthday party for her young daughter, I almost snorted into the receiver.

I said, "A birthday party in December? Don't she know Santa's coming in a couple of weeks?" Mrs. Forde laughed right along with me. I continued, knowing that she'd listen for as long as I talked. "For my birthday when I was a girl, my mama swiped the kitchen table clean with her arm sleeve so that me and my brothers and sisters and cousins could sit around a nice, cleared-off space and eat a Pillsbury birthday cake, yellow with chocolate frosting. If it was a lucky year, she added sprinkles on top. That was my birthday party."

Mrs. Forde was always handing out favors like she was the Queen of Good Will. Of course, I'd never question her judgment but couldn't help wondering whether she was getting paid back in a good way. One of my cousins used to do all kinds of favors for the crowd he hung out with, and he ended up dead. Shot in the back.

"Maybe it's because we don't have children, Tillie," Mrs. Forde said. "If we did, maybe we'd spoil them as rotten as we could."

No need to worry about that, I thought. My chance of being a mother died when Jimmy did.

Mrs. Forde thanked me and gave me the address so I could write it down.

We had to take the Metra train since this house was up north in a suburb close to the lake. I almost called Mrs. Forde back to cancel but didn't.

After Nicolette and me got off the train, we walked eight blocks to the house. Snow covered every inch of the ground, making it look like it was the North Pole, a North Pole full of mansions. Unlike my neighborhood, every last sidewalk was cleared off.

The woman who answered the door didn't look much older than Nicolette. She was nice and all, but I thought to myself how in the world did she get herself into a house like that. Nicolette was her silent self while I asked this girl what cleaning she wanted done. I told her I wasn't blowing up no balloons and she smiled, her teeth as white and smooth as the snow outside.

Later in the day, I caught Nicolette standing at the doorway of the girl's bedroom with her dusting rag in her hand, watching the young mother read to her daughter in a bed. I peeked through the doorway. Nicolette had one of her expressions on her face. I touched her arm and said, "Come on. Time to get back to work, okay?"

When we finished cleaning the house, the girl gave us a big tip. Made me feel uncomfortable even though I appreciated her gesture. I thanked her for the money. Nicolette seemed like she was somewhere else so I nudged her to get a thank you from her. When I took the money, I noticed that her fingers didn't have no diamonds or large rings on them to match the size of her house. Only one gold wedding band.

We piled on our coats, scarves, and gloves, and I put up my hood and tightened the string under my chin so that only my face showed. I couldn't stand it when my ears got cold. Nicolette put on her black wool hat, and we walked outside into dark air that felt like our nostrils was sucking air made of molasses. It wasn't quite dark yet. Our train was leaving in seventeen minutes. All I wanted was to get home to my apartment and take me a hot bath.

We turned the corner, and every last one of them houses had all kinds of colored lights wrapped around bushes and thick evergreen wreaths on their front doors. These people sure knew how to decorate for the birth of Jesus.

I told Nicolette, pointing to a stone house, "Look at that. Ain't that pretty?" A single candlelight glowed in each of the windows.

She nodded.

In the next yard, we passed a snowman. He stood all bare, had no eyes, no nose, no twigs for arms. I wondered if nobody taught them kids up here how to stick a carrot in a ball of snow. I asked Nicolette, "They have that "Frosty the Snowman" song in your country?"

She shook her head, her eyes a little more shiny than usual.

I started singing the song for her. We walked another block or two and I got the feeling that she didn't like my singing, so I switched to hummin' it. Ahead of us on the sidewalk, a group of teenaged boys stood clumped together. They wore leather coats and skull caps. I stopped humming and wanted to holler out for them to move so we could get by them, but when we got to where they was standing, I could see that they weren't about to move for us. Puffed air came from their mouths like they was smoking.

I tugged on Nicolette's arm and said, "Come on." We moved around them and had to step into piles of snow on the edge of the sidewalk. Them boys just stood there.

One of the boys yelled, "Hey, nigger mama, how'd you get this far north? Someone let you out of your pen?" The boys' laughter rang out in the cold air.

I grabbed Nicolette's arm and said, "Keep walking." But the slick pavement prevented us from walking faster.

"Niggers must not have ears," he said, following behind us. "Didn't you hear me?"

My skin got all prickly. Then he said to Nicolette, "You must be Snow White." I could hear the snap of the word *white* when he said it. "Why'd you exchange your seven dwarfs for this black bitch?" A new round of laughter from the boys. They thought that one was real funny.

I didn't hear if Nicolette responded. Someone shoved me from behind and I fell forward to the sidewalk, its freezing cement scraping my face. Nicolette knelt beside me. Like they was animals, the boys circled us.

"Tillie, are you hurt?" I felt her arm across my back.

Then one of them kicked me, a sharp pain in my shoulder. I moaned. Warm spittle hit my cheek and I wiped it off. "Nicolette, get out of here." No telling what these boys were capable of. "Go back to that house."

I felt Nicolette's arm tighten around my back. From the corner of my eye, I saw her head lift and it looked almost like she was smelling the air.

"Nigger lover, you better listen to your friend. Get the fuck out of here. We'll make sure big mama gets back home," he said. "Safe and sound."

I ain't scared of much, always letting faith take over fear, but I never been on the ground like this before with someone standing above me kicking and spitting at me.

Some car honked its horn and I thought the boys might run off.

Then I heard Nicolette let out a fierce scream, a scream like she must of been holding it in for a long time. I prayed they hadn't hurt her. I never did hear a girl scream like that before. I seen Nicolette lunge at the boy and seen his white bare palm stretched in front of him to stop Nicolette from coming at him. But she went at him anyways. A couple of seconds later, his voice, shaky this time, shot out at her. "You crazy bitch, you bit me. You bit my fucking hand." He stood back, one hand holding the other, his eyes wide open and disbelieving of the situation. Nicolette was on her knees, her breath frantic and choppy. She looked up at the boy. Then she slowly stood up and stood completely still, like she was some kind of statue. Dazed and looking all confused, she wiped her mouth with the back of her glove. Sweet Jesus, if I had to see a drop of that boy's blood on her mouth, I would've gotten sick right then. Nicolette, her voice hoarse, said, "Leave her alone."

I heard the car horn again and the boy ran toward it yelling, "Fucking bitches." Nicolette lowered herself beside me. She was crying now. We huddled together on the sidewalk. She lowered her head against my face. We stayed on the ground, our bodies tight against one another. No one bothered to see if we was okay, not that many people was walking around, but I seen a few shadows moving in the distance against the snow. Nicolette's crying turned to sobs, the kind that come from a person's deep insides, the way I cried when Jimmy died.

I said, "I'm okay now, just a little shook up. Come on, there's no sense crying like this. Those boys are gone."

She looked at me not saying a word. Then like something been lifted from my eyes, I knew that she wasn't crying only for me.

After some time, she quieted down. We helped each other stand up.

"You know you can't go around biting people like that," I told her. "You'll get yourself rabies from a street rat like that."

Then we started walking toward the train station without a sound.

~~~

After dawn, in the new light of morning, my mother died.

Papa wanted his wife buried in *Zentrafriedhog,* the cemetery that kept the bones of Beethoven and Schubert. I only wanted Mama to be protected from the rains and winds, snow and ice that would come year after year upon her grave. I told myself that in the autumn, trees would drop red leaves like kisses upon her tombstone, and in the spring, wild violets would grow beside her to keep her company.

At the funeral Mass, Papa and I entered the first pew. When I knelt, my stiff black dress that Fräulein Elstein had bought me for the funeral scratched my knees. I kept expecting Mama at any moment to come into our pew and kneel beside me.

When the priest swung the censer over Mama's casket, incense was released and its harsh odor, reminiscent of burning silk, reached me.

We were driven in a black automobile to the cemetery. Outside the window, mist clung to the countless monuments and stone crosses. The car moved slowly down the long road and stopped where the earth had been opened for my mother.

Fräulein Elstein, our neighbors, and Father Vogl circled the casket adorned with yellow roses, Mama's favorite. As they had in life, both my parents' families abandoned us in death.

I stood next to Papa, stoic and silent. My legs quivered and I was afraid that they would fail to keep me upright during the burial. I held onto Papa's arm, dug my fingers into his overcoat. Father Vogl spoke of salvation and of God's eternal love, but his words gave me no comfort.

One of Papa's friends, a former singer in the State Opera Chorus, waited for the nod from Father Vogl. After the final prayers were said, the man looked upward, and began to sing "Ave Maria." I watched the man sing Schubert's hymn to my mother, concentrating on the movement of his lips, the lifting of his chest, the inflection of his voice, all to keep me from running to her.

When the service ended, I was left alone with my father who fell deeper into despair, into a depth that we both owned, but one that he would not share with me.

Weeks after Mama's death, the four occupying countries signed a treaty declaring Austria's independence. In autumn, the last of Red Army soldiers would leave our country. They had been there ten years. They would leave Austria for their frozen soil. Other countries remained less fortunate; there the Russians would stay.

I waited for my mother's voice. I waited in the early hours of morning for her to wake me for school, and in the evenings, I waited for her to call me to our table. Her voice had been soft, melodic, but in truth, I had forgotten its sound.

An afternoon when I returned home from school, the air startled me with fragrant smells of *apfelstrudel* and coffee. A voice spoke to me from my parents' bedroom. "Hello?"

Fräulein Elstein walked into the kitchen; her hands held a white towel. "How was your day?"

She gestured for me to sit at our table and went to prepare a hot chocolate for me.

Again, she asked about my day, her tone stern. "I asked about your day."

"It was fine," I said.

"That's better."

In a few minutes, she slid the cup toward me, the sound from the cup lingering like the soft screech of a bird. She smiled stiffly and then brought two plates of strudel and two forks. She sat down.

"After you eat, you must practice the violin. I promised your father that you would keep to your schedule." Her skin looked as stale as old bread. She bit into the strudel. I looked down at my strudel, a stone upon my plate. A sour liquid rose in my throat.

"I bought the ingredients for *gulashsuppe.* You like that, correct?"

I nodded afraid that if I spoke, I would become sick at the table.

"Well, if you're not going to eat," she said with a sharp sting to her words, "you can help me move my things into the bedroom."

She stood up and I followed her to where the boxes were piled.

I carried one of her boxes into my parents' bedroom, expecting Mama's scent of jasmine to reach me. The photograph of my parents at their wedding ceremony had been removed from the bureau. A crystal bell sat in its place. I set the box next to it, pushing the bell close to the edge of the dresser, wanting to see it shatter on the floor.

Fräulein Elstein handed me a thin book. "Your mother loved Blake."

It was a book of his poems.

"With her voice, she could recite these with near perfection. I miss her too, Nicolette."

The nausea returned and a lightness swept through my head. "Fräulein Elstein, I don't feel well," I said to her. "My stomach hurts."

She looked unsure of what to say or do.

"Bring me the other box," she said and took a step closer to me. "Then you may rest before you practice." She squeezed my arm, a little too hard. "Perhaps you can shorten your practice time, only for today," she said and winked at me. "I won't tell your father."

Later that night, when Papa and Fräulein Elstein were in my parents' bed, thoughts of my mother and the Russian soldier stirred in the dark. Did she care for the soldier and not Papa? Why had Mama not told him? Why had he not protected her? Why had the soldier chosen Mama? I prayed that sleep would take me from these thoughts but was taunted by images of Mama's eyes softening toward the soldier, of her face warming to his presence. Had I seen her touch his sleeve for no reason?

I tried to recall my mother's saints and the stories she had told me about them: Saint Cecilia, Saint Monica, and Joan of Arc. I turned on the small lamp beside my bed and pulled out the heavy book Mama had given me on my tenth birthday, her last gift to me. In its pages I found a reproduction of Reni's painting of Saint Cecilia, the patron saint of musicians. Reni had painted a young Cecilia holding the violin in front of her with her left hand, and in her right hand, the bow, crossing the center of the instrument. Cecilia's dark eyes looked upward; her face, pale and soft; her head wrapped with an ivory cloth. Mama had told me that for three continuous days Saint Cecilia sang to God in the midst of her dying. For her faith, she was granted an incorrupt body after her burial—a body untouched by decay.

When I turned out the light, I saw my mother's body buried under layers of soil and clay.

Two years after Mama's death, Papa received a telegram from my grandmother saying she would be in Vienna for business. She wanted to meet with Papa. As if to lure him, my grandmother promised to bring personal belongings of my mother's. Papa refused to respond to the letter, but I wanted whatever she had of Mama's—a comb, her handkerchief, a photograph of Mama when she was my age. After my continued pleadings, Papa's arm waved me off, and he ordered Fräulein Elstein to accompany me. Her letter instructed Papa to meet her at a *kaffeehaus* close to Saint Stephen's Cathedral for *jause*. She told him to meet her on Tuesday at four o'clock.

Though it was a weekday, Fräulein Elstein and I entered the *kaffeehaus* in our Sunday clothes. Before today I had never entered one, had only walked past countless times peering through the windowpanes of glass at the desserts displayed like miniature pieces of artwork.

Inside, we were surrounded by glass and wood and light. Smells lingered and wrapped around me— roasted coffee beans, cigarette smoke, *tortes* baked from butter dough. Marble tables held small silver trays with white ceramic cups and water glasses. Men sat reading newspapers, smoking, while women gathered in groups of two or three, talking and laughing, something I was not accustomed to. Near a window, an older woman sat alone, her head rigid as she watched us. A small black hat perched atop her silver hair; its sheer netting covered her face.

Fräulein Elstein gripped my hand as we walked toward the woman. She said, "There's your grandmother. Now mind yourself, Nicolette."

At the table, Fräulein Elstein remained standing and nodded to my grandmother. "Frau Dreher. Good afternoon."

"I expected to see Josef, Fräulein Elstein," my grandmother said. "Tell me, it is still Fräulein?"

"Yes," Fräulein Elstein said, her eyes fixed on my grandmother's face. "Josef is working today. Nicolette asked for her mother's things, so I brought her. I help Josef with the child." She paused. "Nicolette told me she has never met you. Could this be true?"

My grandmother did not answer but gestured for us to sit across from her in the booth. The seat's red velvet-like material was the same color as the inside of my violin case, the same color as the new red wine Papa drank. My fingertips rested on the marble table. Fräulein Elstein cleared her throat and I dropped my hands into my lap. My grandmother removed her hat. The glare of the late afternoon sun shone through the picture window; my grandmother's blue eyes—those I knew; they were my mother's—stood out against her skin, the color of the paste we used at school. Above red painted lips, her wrinkles looked like violin strings pulled too tightly.

She studied my face. "You look little of your mother. Rather you seem to resemble me. How old are you now?"

"Twelve," I answered, unsettled by her comment.

My grandmother's eyes did not move from my face. "Is that so? And what about your father? How is he?"

Fräulein Elstein answered for me. "Josef is fine."

"I've heard that he is not very well, that he drinks too much, yes?" my grandmother asked, though I could not tell which of us she was questioning.

Again, Fräulein Elstein answered. "He works at the factory. And he composes."

"I always warned Paulina of his ideas and of his drink, but it was no use. And you, child," turning her glassy eyes back upon me, "you must play the violin."

I did not know if it was a question. I nodded; an urge rose within me to speak out—to tell her how I was required to keep an extended practice schedule, some days for hour upon hour behind a locked door, that my fingertips were numb and reddened. My eyes met Fräulein Elstein's. "Yes, I play."

Fräulein Elstein said, "Frau Dreher, who gives you this information? You live far from here. You failed to attend your daughter's funeral—"

"—Let me remind you, Fräulein Elstein," my grandmother said, her voice slapping against the sweetened air but stifled enough to avoid a scene, "Paulina and Josef chose against our heritage and only hope at the time. And her funeral...even if I had tried to come, there were far too many blockades at the Russian zones." She took in a sharp breath and waved to the waiter. "You remember how it was?"

Dressed in a black jacket and pants, a white dress shirt and black bowtie, the waiter approached our table. His gestures stiff, he said to Fräulein Elstein, "May I bring you something to drink?"

"Only water for the two of us," she said. "Thank you."

The waiter's eyes scanned us momentarily, his lips tightened before he slightly bowed. He asked my grandmother, "Would you like me to bring you your *linzertorte* now?"

"Yes, I'm ready." She asked Fräulein Elstein, "You'll allow me to order something for my granddaughter?"

I touched the cold marble, my fingers moving in small circles.

Fräulein Elstein sighed. "A *mélange* for me, and for Nicolette, a hot cocoa. I don't want her dinner to be spoiled."

The waiter left to retrieve my grandmother's t*orte* from the kitchen.

My grandmother said, "I hope he gave her beautiful funeral. Did he have enough money?"

I wanted to run from the table so that I would not have to hear about my mother's funeral. At the table next to us, I watched a woman as she lifted a fork with chocolate cake on it to her mouth. I imagined its taste, thick with sugar, dense with cream, on my tongue. Under the table, my legs swung back and forth, timed and exact like the metronome that Papa used at our lessons.

Fräulein Elstein said, "Let's not discuss that in front of Nicolette. We came for her mother's belongings."

"Very well," my grandmother said. She smiled at me. "Did your mother ever talk of our family?"

"No," I said, "not much."

Her smile stiffened into an unpleasant smile as she looked out the window, her gaze following a man walking toward the cathedral.

The waiter returned and set the silver tray in front of her, the *linzertorte* perfectly centered on the plate. Black current jam filled the layers, glistened along the edges. Like a veil waiting to be lifted, confectionery sugar clung to the lattice pastry. With swollen fingers, she picked up the white napkin, unfolded it, and placed it on her lap. I sat motionless and watched her take a drink from her water glass. My hands, hidden under the table, pressed together until my entwined fingers hurt. Kept loose and free, they would have seized her *torte* and pushed it into my mouth.

In a few minutes, the waiter returned with another silver tray, holding a *mélange* and a hot cocoa and two glasses of chilled water. He placed the tray in front of us.

No one spoke. When my grandmother finished, she lifted a wooden box from underneath the table and slid it toward me. The lid of the box was painted with liquid-red camellias.

She said, "This is what you came for. Open it."

The wooden box held a photograph of my mother as a girl, a rosary made of crystal beads, and at the bottom, letters tied with ribbon. I closed the lid of the wooden box and thanked my grandmother.

She said, "Your mother asked me to mail the box to her. I told her that she had to come home to retrieve it." Her hand waved to the waiter. "But she never returned home."

"Like Joan of Arc," I said quietly.

"What did you say?" she said.

"Joan of Arc never returned home before she died," I said.

"Well, what does that matter?" she said.

I said, meeting her eyes, "Mama told me stories of the saints at bedtime. Joan of Arc was Mama's favorite. She told me that she saved her country with soldiers and that we were saving ours with the rosary."

But my grandmother wasn't interested in my remark and began counting her schillings. She placed them on the top of the slip of paper the waiter had left. Reaching for her hat, she arranged it on her head. Mama's eyes became veiled once more. My grandmother said, "I would like to visit Paulina's grave."

Fräulein Elstein lifted her cup to her lips. I heard her swallow the liquid.

My grandmother said, "Fräulein Elstein, we all have our sins, do we not? And if you must know, I have received mercy from our Lord. Under the circumstances, under the pressure of our country, I did what I had to do. To say the very least, I've certainly paid the price with the loss of my husband. Please understand." She lowered her voice and said, "I simply want to pay my respects to my daughter."

Fräulein Elstein lowered her cup on the table.

From the back corner of the *kaffeehaus*, silverware crashed against the tiled floor and a water glass shattered. In one breath, I said, "My mother is buried in *Zentralfriedhof*. The tram will take you to the main entrance."

Fräulein Elstein's fingers gripped her cup.

I said, "*Oma,* I can give you the location."

My grandmother pulled out a paper from her purse and handed me a pen and the paper. "Write it down," she said, "please." Then she stood erect and took the paper from me, folded it, placed it in her purse. "Let me know, Nicolette, if there is ever anything I can do for you." She paused then looked at Fräulein Elstein. "You should at least buy her a pastry before you leave."

She walked away from our table.

~~~

The two of us kept cleaning together and I think we both felt something had changed between us, a shift in the atmosphere, kind of like you feel when one season changes to the next. Nicolette came to Mama's with me for Christmas. Blanche was her own skeptical self, complaining to Mama that I was foolish for bringing her, but Mama said if you wouldn't bring someone into your home at Christmas, then when would you? Nicolette was like a celebrity and—I tell you—that girl liked it. The kids, especially Monique, kept buzzing around her like bumble bees, bringing her punch or a plate of cookies. And once I seen little Pearl come up to her and rub the back of Nicolette's hand, like the white might rub off.

Before Nicolette left, she handed me a cassette tape in my hand, said it was her playing some song, something about D major, by a guy named Packabell. Later that night, in my apartment, I put the tape in my cassette recorder and listened.

Nicolette could play all right. So good that I thought she should get herself in one of them orchestra groups they had in the loop.

The rest of winter was nothing but snow, wind, and cold. Not much to say about it except I spent a lot of time talking to my pastor, working out in my head what happened to me on that icy sidewalk. Me and Nicolette never did talk about it again.

Then in spring King got shot and the streets of Chicago raged.

I was able to get to Mama, almost half out of her mind being closest to it all. When I got to Madison near her place, there were sirens and breaking glass, the smell of fire, and people taking armfuls from stores like Judgment Day was no reality. A boy, looked like he no more than twelve, walked right by me with a case of beer wrapped in his arms, like he got a package from Santa. If circumstances was different, I would of grabbed it right from him.

When I arrived at her apartment, I hugged Mama tight. She said, "Why's this happening, Tillie? Why they doing this?"

"Don't know, Mama," I said. "Don't know. Upset about King. Don't make no sense." After I set my purse on the table and got me a Tab, I pulled the Bible down from the shelf and we started saying the Psalms out loud. It calmed her some, but each time another siren went off in the distance she would look up at me, she like the child and me the mama.

Each of my siblings called to see if Mama was okay. They knew I'd stay with her since I was the one with no family. Each of them spoke with their own mixture of disbelief, anger and fear.

Once I got Mama fed and settled in her chair, I checked in on Nicolette calling her from the kitchen phone. Some female answered the phone at the boarding house not understanding me, acting like she under the influence of some kind of substance. Finally, she got what I was saying and who I was asking for. A few minutes later, Nicolette's voice came on.

She said, "Hello?"

"Don't you think about leaving the house tonight. Stay put until—"

"—What do you mean?" Nicolette asked.

"Don't you know? Martin Luther King Jr. is dead and people be crazy in the streets."

"Who?"

Speaking louder through the receiver, I said, "Martin Luther King Jr. is dead. People be setting fires and acting crazy. Now you listen to me. Stay inside until I call you."

"Tillie, I do not understand. Where are you?"

"At Mama's. Praying for this to end." I tried to keep my voice steady for Mama's sake but I could hear it starting to shake. "Chaos is everywhere."

"Nothing is outside here." Nicolette paused on the other end of the line. "I planned to meet someone later tonight. His jazz quartet plays at 9 o'clock."

"Girl, you got plugs in your ears? We got us hell outside our doors and you worried about getting out, listening to some guy blow his trumpet?" I gripped the receiver tighter. "It's not that professor you been talking about more than you know, is it?"

"He plays the piano, not the trumpet," Nicolette said. "I promised him—"

"—I don't care if you promised President Johnson. I'll call you when it's safe." There was no sound on her end. "Nicolette, you there?"

"Yes."

"You don't need to be messing around with no teacher. He probably got himself a wife and kids on the side. You hear me?"

There was a pause on the other end of the line. "Yes."

"Goodbye then." I hung up and went back to Mama.

When it was time for bed, Mama asked that I stay in her room. I moved the chair close to the bed and sat with her until she fell asleep.

And since I got the sense to know when a girl is telling me one thing and her voice another, I went to the kitchen and called the boarding house again. This time some old woman answered the phone.

"Is Nicolette there?"

"Nicolette?" the woman said, pronouncing each syllable like it was a separate word.

"The girl with the German accent."

"Oh yes, such a lovely girl. I saw her leave a while back. I don't remember what time. I've spent most of the day here in the foyer watching out the window for the cardinal but now it's dark out there. He usually rests on the lower branch of the white birch." The woman kept talking. "I love his red feathers, how his face looks like it's painted black. You know my husband Carl had red hair, but not from eating holly berries like the cardinal." A small laugh over the line.

It was too late for this woman to be up. "Is she back?"

"Oh, I don't think so. I've been sitting here most of the evening, except to use the washroom. She looked pretty. I think she was going to a dance."

"There ain't no dance tonight. You better get yourself to bed."

"I was just thinking of walking back to my room. I like to watch Johnny."

She paused. "My son, Stan, hasn't called for a long time. I hope he's okay."

"I'm sure he is." I didn't think the mayor's shoot-to-kill order would involve her son.

"He doesn't like the smell of nursing homes," she said. "He says they're too expensive. That's why I'm here."

"I really got to go."

"Oh, okay. It's been nice talking to you. What's your name?"

I hesitated. "Tillie," I said. "Good night now."

The woman said, "My name is Ida."

I heard Mama call from the bedroom. "Tillie?"

"Ida, I have to go. It was nice talking to you. Good night."

"Goodnight, Tillie."

I walked back to the bedroom and Mama was sitting up in bed with the Bible in her lap, reciting a psalm. Her voice didn't hold an ounce of conviction. "O Lord, because you have lifted me up and have not let my enemies triumph over me...I cried out to you, and you restored me to health."

I squeezed her hand and sat beside her on the bed. "We got to pray louder, Mama. Don't think He hearing us."

The next time I seen Nicolette I didn't take the time to scold her. At her age, she be old enough to take care of herself and who she runs around with. But I noticed right away she looked different; the tightness left her face, like someone looks just before they are about to smile. Even her hair was looser in its bun. She wore this shirt that pulled at her chest and blue jeans that flared so much at the bottom I thought she'd trip and fall. And her lips looked like she smeared a tangerine all over them. Almost made me laugh, but I kept quiet. I could of used a good laugh instead of thinking about all the bad that happened over the weekend. At least no one we knew got shot or arrested.

Up to now whenever we cleaned, Nicolette never asked me much about anything. Maybe one to two questions, but usually I was the one doing the asking and she the one giving me her half-answers.

Nicolette said, "You had a husband?"

Now it was my turn to look at her all strange.

"I told you that."

We was dusting in the parlor, that's what the woman of the house called it—the parlor—like she was an English woman expecting the Queen to drop

67

by for tea any minute. Jimmy wrote me telling me how them English people liked their tea. I guess some people can't help wanting bigger lives than they got.

Nicolette said, "How did you meet him?"

"In New Orleans." The first time I seen him flashed quick in my mind. "Visiting some relatives that lived there after my high school graduation. I got good grades so Mama let me go. We was at a church picnic, and it was so hot and humid you felt like you was swimming in air." I paused. "I told my cousin someday that boy with a mischievous grin watching me from under those droopy branches would marry me. The next year I accepted his proposal, but only if we would live in Chicago near my family after he got out of the service. Jimmy told me, 'I'd follow you anywhere, Sugar, as long as you learn to make my grandmama's *quinjombo.*'"

"How did you know?"

"Know what?"

"That you would marry him."

"I don't know. Some things you just know."

She looked at me but didn't say nothing.

"But there was no way I was going to stay in that swamp. Don't know how anyone lives there, sharing your space with reptiles. Ain't no place to raise babies. Jimmy once told me that when he was a boy, he and his friends swam in the bayou with alligators. But Jimmy was that way. No wonder they sent him to fight Hitler." I started dusting the grandfather clock and it started to go off. If I had one of these things in my

68

place, that loud ringing would get on my last nerve. I waited until it was done then turned to Nicolette and said, "You'd like it down there, there's a mess of Catholics around, that and a bunch of voodoo people. Jimmy loved it all." I smiled. "But he loved me more."

I stopped moving my dust rag. It felt good to talk about him. Nicolette was leaning up against the doorjamb with that ridiculous color still on her lips. If I had a tissue in my pocket, I would of walked up right to her and wiped it off. It was too much for her. Instead, I told her to keep working. She moved toward the small table with curlicue legs, just the size for holding a pot of tea.

Nicolette said, "Tell me about Jimmy."

"You want to know about Jimmy?" I said, "Okay then. He was always surprising me with something different. He knew about things." I sprayed blue glass cleaner on the face of the clock, appreciating its antiseptic smell. "One night, soon after our wedding, Jimmy told me that I was as rare and beautiful as the ivory-billed woodpecker. I forget its real name. He seen one in the bayou the summer before and was proud as could be that no one else did. Guess there's not a lot of them around. Told me that it must have been a male because of the red feathers sticking straight up on his skull. Said that he had to go look it up at the library. So I said to him, if you telling me that I remind you of a large male bird, how you think you getting on my side of the bed tonight?" I stopped wiping the glass, not intending to share a detail I should of kept to myself. Nicolette's rag continued to move back and forth across the wood.

I remembered Jimmy's low laugh that rolled through his throat, then the feel of him pulling at my shirt. He was always pulling at my shirt.

"Okay," I said. "You really want to know what Jimmy was like? He was like pudding. An endless spoonful of pudding."

"I do not understand."

"You shouldn't. Not until you find a man worth keeping."

"You can marry again," she said.

There was no earthly way to explain how I still ached for that man, how the pain inside me was like a river that slowed but never stopped. No more weddings for me. I bent to put the window cleaner in the bucket. I shook my head. "A husband is a once in a lifetime experience for me." With the bucket in hand, I started walking to the next room. "And I done had mine."

~~~

Winters and summer passed like collected stones in the jar under my bed. At night, my hands wandered over my body, my fingers finding new flesh that had thickened my legs and breasts. In daylight, my fingers traced the silvery streaks that stretched across the skin on my upper legs and hips. Some days a sudden tightness gripped my mind, and a sharp tongue lashed at Fräulein Elstein, and I feared that a hint of madness had settled within me. When my monthly blood came, to soothe the pain that coiled inside, I pressed and kneaded my skin with my palms, curled my legs to my chest, wrapped my arms around my knees. When the pain did not ease, I dipped rags into boiling water, rung them out, and placed them low on my stomach. Scraps of rags that I used to catch my blood I threw out with the refuse. Fräulein Elstein knew none of this.

Mama's book of poems, *Songs of Innocence and Songs of Experience,* stayed under my pillow. Each week, to learn English quicker than the other students in my class, I brought home a paper sack full of books from the library: *Learn English in Thirty Days; English: The Proper Way; English Is Quite Easy.* While other girls my age looked at themselves in front of their mirrors, wrapping and curling their hair in ways they were sure boys would like, I looked at myself in the mirror, watching my lips move, listening to my uttered sounds. My voice slowed, like an adagio, to capture each of Blake's words. By the time I was fifteen years old, I had committed his poems to memory in their original English. I quietly recited this poem that I believed was Mama's favorite while I walked to school most mornings.

Piping down the valleys wild
Piping songs of pleasant glee
On a cloud I saw a child.
And he laughing said to me.

Pipe a song about a Lamb;
So I piped with merry chear,
Piper, pipe that song again—
So I piped, he wept to hear.

Drop thy pipe, thy happy piper
Sing thy songs of happy chear,
So I sung the same again
While he wept with joy to hear

Piper, sit thee down and write
In a book that all may read—
So he vanish'd from my sight.
And I pluck'd a hollow reed.

And I made a rural pen,
And I stain'd the water clear,
And I wrote my happy songs
Every child may joy to hear.

Most days after school, I walked alone through the
streets. Anya, and my few other friends, understood
that I was different from them and did not ask me to
go with them to the park near our building. On my
walks, many times I caught glimpses of Mama. One
autumn afternoon I watched my mother's body turn
down *Tuchlauben.* The woman carried herself with
sudden familiarity to me: elegant shoulders, her head
slightly tilted to the left, a stride that matched Mama's
pace. The shade of her hair was too dark; still, I
followed. Beside the woman, my heart pulsed as if I ran
the distance to her. I turned and looked and saw not
the face of my mother, but that of a stranger.

"*Grüss Gott,*" the woman said with a polite nod.

"*Grüss Gott,*" I said and took a step away from
her.

Later that afternoon, instead of going home to practice
the violin, I found myself south of the *Ringstrausse,* at
the Heroes' Monument of the Red Army. The
foundation's specks of red stone glinted in the sun. On
top of the large monument stood a bronzed Russian
soldier, the unknown soldier. Stalin's engraved words

on a plaque commended his Red Army for their victory, their liberation of Vienna. I walked around the monument with slow steps. I bent down and scraped a handful of dirt from the ground and threw it at the Russian soldier, the drops of soil scattering into the air but not touching him.

Those of us who remembered called the monument by its true name, the monument of the unknown plunderer.

Like a monotonous composition, my life held the same tempo from year to year. In my last year of *Gymnasium*, I passed a set of examinations, earned my diploma, and began study at the Art Academy. In the middle of my third year, I mailed a letter to my grandmother and awaited her reply.

A February day when the wind stayed restless, Papa and I were home alone. I walked into his bedroom; he sat at his small table, composing, his back to me. I touched his shoulder, but he did not turn around. His hair, streaked with grey, was kept too long for a man. I placed a small box of marzipan with four pieces of miniature fruit inside on the table. Pages of Schubert's *Unfinished Symphony* were spread around him with Papa's notes written over those of Schubert's.

I said, "Papa, you're working too long again. I brought you marzipan."

"How can composers rest," Papa said, "when there is music to create? Schubert must have sensed, when he held a torch at Beethoven's burial, that his life would be cut short. Compositions flew from him at such a rapid pace."

"Papa," I said, "I need to talk with you."

Ignoring my words, he continued. "Did you know that Beethoven once said of Schubert's music that it must have come from the divine light. And now—how many years later—I have the privilege of completing it!"

"What do you mean?" I said.

"His third movement finally came to me."

Against Papa's window, sleet began to fall. I sat on his bed. My fingers touched the white coverlet, one that Fraulein Elstein had brought with her, one that when I was younger, I had wanted to cut into shreds.

"Papa, what do you mean? He intended only two movements."

"Nonsense!" Papa said. "And how would you know?"

From my satchel, I removed an envelope. "I need to read a letter to you."

He turned in his chair to look at me. "What did you say?"

"I have a letter," I said pulling the ivory paper from the envelope, refusing to look at him. "It's from *Oma.*"

"Why?" he said. "Why would she write you?"

When I did not answer him, he turned his back to me. "Go ahead," he said.

Written in blue ink, my grandmother's handwriting was small and slanted. I heard Papa shift in his chair. In a quiet voice, I read the letter.

Dear Nicolette,   *2 February 1967*
*   I received your letter and must admit how surprised I was by its arrival and content. The reason for my delay is that I needed time to fully consider your request. Prior to now, I doubted that I would ever see you again. Your mother and I had a conflicted relationship. How she loved to debate me—even as a young child. She seemed to want something from me that I could not give her. When Paulina was young and ill, she would call for her English governess in the middle of the night, never for me.*

*   The annexation and then the war led to our final separation. Her father and I did what we thought was aligned with God's will. Only now do I see that we were wrong.*

*   I must ask—what does your father think of your request?*

*   I presume that Chicago has fine universities but thought that New York City would offer more opportunity in musical study. But what do I know of such things, living in the countryside of Austria?*

*   Your request reminds me of your mother. She wanted to study in London, somehow developed a keen sense of the English, especially their writers. Paulina was never content with her reality. As a child, she lived out her dreams and thought that life should reflect the magical. Whereas I have always believed in*

the concrete, in the actual matter of things, Paulina
always believed in ideas, in the possibility of things.

From your letter, I expect that you have received
appropriate placement at the university and are only
awaiting my response. Once you have your father's
approval, let me know where I should wire the money.
And then, please write me when you are settled there.
I would like to stay in contact with you.

In some way, I feel this is a way to make amends
with my daughter.

Yours truly,

Oma

The door opened and Fräulein Elstein strode into
the bedroom still wearing her coat. "Why are you
disturbing your father?"

I stood up as if I were a child again. "I needed to
ask him a question."

"Josef, I need her help in the kitchen."

Papa looked at me. "She can stay with me."

Fräulein Elstein turned and left. Within seconds,
a pan banged against the stove.

"Papa, I should have asked you first. I never
thought the university would accept me...but they did.
I will stay for only a year then will come home."

He stood with his back to me again, his head
bowed to look at the score. As if he were a
Kapellmeister and I his audience, he lifted his right
arm, swinging it back and forth through thick air.

He lowered his arm.

Without turning around, he said, "You are willing to accept money from a Nazi?"

"*Oma's* money is the only way for me to study in America," I said.

He turned to look at me. "Do you know what you are asking of me?" He raised his left hand and shook it. "Look at this!"

"I'm sorry, Papa. But that was a long time ago," I said. "I have always done what you wanted. I have always played the violin, for you." My voice rose to a level that I had never used with him before. "This is what I want!"

"To leave Vienna and study music in the middle of America?" He laughed. "That's absurd! Why America?"

"Everyone wants to go to America!"

"There is nothing for you there."

Sleet fell against the window like small slivers of broken glass.

"And what is *here* for me?" Anger opened inside of me like uncontrollable flames. "Unless I hold a violin in my hands, you pay no attention to me. I play only because you cannot. And now, every day, I watch you do this!" I picked up the score, shaking the pages. "You act as if you are a composer, changing Schubert's compositions." I threw the sheets on the floor.

Papa did not move but kept his eyes on the pages.

I continued, "You cannot change what he has written. He is dead, Papa, dead like Mama." I took in

78

a deep breath, unable to stop the words that followed. "Because we did not protect her."

He looked at me. "Protect her?" His eyes were the color I imagined the center of the ocean to be.

I said, "From the soldier."

"What solider?" he said.

"The Russian soldier."

"No, Nicolette. There was no soldier."

"Yes, Papa, he—"

"—No."

"Papa," I said, "that's not the truth."

"Truth?" His voice became so low that I could barely hear him. "What is truth?"

Papa picked up pages of the score from the floor and sat back down at his desk, his back to me again.

He said, "Go help in the kitchen. I have work to finish."

"But, Papa—"

His voice raised, he said, "Nicolette, you will not go to America. Now leave."

~~~

The Chicago summer was hot and sticky. So sticky a wet film of sweat stayed on my skin the whole month of July. I thought Nicolette would go back to Vienna as soon as her semester was over, but when I questioned her about it, she said her flight was for the beginning of September. Glad we had another month because I wasn't ready for her to go home.

In one of those rare moments of her sharing something, she told me that her father had been moved to a sanatorium, one close to the woods where Beethoven used to walk. That Elstein woman had to take him there. I could tell that she was bothered by it but guess not enough to go back to Vienna right away. This time I said nothing.

Mrs. Forde added a couple of days to Nicolette's schedule. But you would've thought she was working five 12-hour shifts the way she kept sitting down taking breaks. Every time I seen her, I'd click my tongue and she'd get back up. Maybe the longer workweek was too much for her. Some people just don't have it in them.

Today we was in the kitchen, and I was scrubbing the stovetop with a sponge trying to get off hardened spaghetti sauce that the woman of the house somehow forgot to clean the night before. I wanted to ask this woman how she got through life not knowing how to take a sponge, a little soap, and some hot water to clean up her own mess. Good Lord.

I looked over at Nicolette and said, "Start sweeping. Them crumbs are as big as cotton balls."

Nicolette just stood there like she didn't hear me.

"What's the matter?" I asked, "You not acting yourself."

"Fräulein Elstein wrote me another letter," she said. "She demands that I come home. Papa is not well." Each word seemed to bring more pain to her face.

"Oh, I'm sorry to hear that."

"Papa asks only for me," she said.

"If he ain't doing good, then you gotta go home."

Nicolette looked out the window.

I said, "What, now you ain't staying on my account? You know me, I'll get along fine." But the truth was that it would tear me up if she left now. Then I seen something come across her face.

She started moving the broom.

My agitation started to burn like acid in my stomach. "It's him. Isn't it? You don't want to leave him," I said. She wouldn't look me in the eye. "You better get yourself back home now. Your dad needs you."

She stopped sweeping and looked right at me. "I cannot go."

81

"Well, why not?" I tried to keep my voice calm like my mama used to when me or my sisters was having one of our female moods. "What it is then? Your professor won't let you go?"

Nicolette stared out the window like the answer to my question was out there instead of in her head. She said, "Philip gave me money last week."

I scrubbed harder at the stovetop. *Philip.* She never used his name with me before. It sounded like a name a professor would have. "Girl, you doing that thing again. Me asking you one question, and you giving me an answer to a different one. Talking to you is about as clear as clay." I gripped the sponge. "Money for what? If he keeping you here, ain't no money for a plane ticket." I moved to the sink and turned on the water to rinse out the sponge.

Nicolette's face was all hard looking.

I started spraying the sink with the hose to rinse out the specks of sauce. Somehow water splashed up in my face and, in a huff, I quick turned off the water. "Hand me that towel over there."

She gave it to me, and I wiped my face. And then it dawned on me. Lord have mercy. How'd I miss this one—her sitting down every half hour, her face as pale as pie crust, them crackers I been seeing her eat. Sweet Jesus. A baby.

"A baby?" I said, out loud this time.

She didn't say a word, but I knew by the look in her eyes that I was right. "What's the money for then?" I said. "Diapers?" I tossed the towel on the counter.

She didn't answer me but instead started sweeping again.

"Well, he better pay for your doctor bills. There's going to be a lot of them."

Her voice low, Nicolette said, "Philip told me to end the baby."

I wasn't sure what I just heard come out of her mouth. "What'd you say?"

She said, "Philip told me to end the baby."

"What do you mean, end the baby? That man told you to have an abortion?"

Nicolette's eyes met mine. "Yes."

"He can't do that. It's your child!"

She said, "Philip told me I am a very good violinist, that a baby would get in the way of my future."

"He can't tell you what to do with *your* baby."

Nicolette said, "I do not know how to be a mother."

"Who does? And it don't matter because you already are. Now listen. You got all them hormones flooding your head. Blanche's second pregnancy made her so crazy she ran away for a night, left her husband and first baby and got herself a hotel room in the loop. Can you imagine paying money for a hotel room because, well I don't know why." I took a breath. "You been to see a doctor?"

Nicolette shook her head.

"Well, we need to get you to one."

The girl looked like she was scared half out of her mind. Good Lord. I went over to her and put my arms around her. She didn't hug me back, but I felt her body soften.

"Come on now. It's gonna be okay," I said, holding her. "Everything's going to be okay."

Nicolette whispered, "I did not know he had a wife."

"I'd hope not," I said too sharply, but quick caught myself. "Now don't you worry yourself about no wife. We got a baby to think of."

~~~

An early morning in late August, I walked to the beach. The sun was low and warm. The wooden bench I sat on faced the water. I took off my sandals and felt the sand under my feet. In the water, a man and woman swam. A breeze moved across my face and I thought of your father. I always thought of him then.

There is a wind in Austria called the *Föhn*. It appears when the skies are blue and clear, when no one expects it. Upon descent, the wind warms dramatically, melts snow and ice along its path. Mama always said you could tell with the *Föhn* was upon us, even without its physical signs. Men and women acted out of character for them.

When I met your father, I felt this wind inside of me.

I was a student in his music theory class. He allowed no instruments in his class, only pen and paper. As I sat in the front row of the class, I felt bare without my violin to hide behind. He spoke in slow sentences, I wanted to believe for my benefit. His lecture vibrated in my ears, and I found it impossible to capture his words on paper. His eyes lingered on my face longer than they should have.

At the end of class when the other students were leaving this classroom, he walked over to me.

"Are you okay?" he said. "You seemed to have a hard time with the notes."

"Yes. I am fine."

He immediately asked where I was from.

"I am from Vienna."

"Oh, I see," he said and smiled. "Come by my office and I can help you with your notes."

"Yes, thank you."

"And then you can tell me about your country. I love Old Vienna."

"Yes," I said.

He said, "What instrument do you play?"

"The violin."

"Perfect," he said.

The next day I went to his office and waited for him.

As I watched the couple swim in the lake, joggers passed behind me on the path. I heard the rhythmic sounds of their feet on the concrete, their heavy breaths. I watched the couple come out of the water and walk to their blanket spread out on the sand. The man reached down for a towel and wrapped it around the woman. It was blue. When they sat down, the woman lifted her face to the rising sun.

The next day on my way to a cleaning job, I passed a newsstand. The front page of the newspaper reported that the Soviet Union invaded Czechoslovakia the day before. It showed a photograph of Russian tanks inside the country. I looked around. Men and women walked

86

to their destinations, smiling and laughing, not reacting to the news. They did not see the Red Army stride down our cobbled streets or see the soldiers' lips, taut and blistered, as we children ran away from them.

They did not see the Russian soldier and my mother.

~~~

We was at one of our easiest cleaning jobs. This woman had moved from New York City a few months ago and worked long hours at some company in the loop. There wasn't much stuff in her apartment, and she had the decency to pick up after herself before we got there. I could of used a few more clients like her.

And after Nicolette had told me about her expecting, she went back to her quiet self.

We was in the woman's bedroom, and it only had a bed and a dresser. No photos were out. Not a one. Nicolette was stripping the bed and I was washing down the walls. This woman was having her bedroom painted this weekend and asked if we could clean the walls.

When I couldn't stand the silence anymore, I said, "You know, I don't mind going to your next appointment with you. Mrs. Forde owes me some time."

Nicolette didn't stop to answer me.

She said, "I can go alone."

I dropped the sponge in the bucket and said, "Why you thinking you need to do this all alone?"

Without looking up at me, she said, "I am alone."

I watched her bundle the bedsheets and leave them on top of the bed.

Not able to let that one go, I said, "Well, what am I then?"

Nicolette turned to look at me. "Why do you like me?"

I paused for a second, not knowing how to respond. "What are you talking about?" I said.

Nicolette pulled out a folded paper from her pocket and walked over to me and held out the paper.

I dried my hands on a rag and took the paper. Unfolding it, I said, "What's this?"

"A letter."

"I can see that it's a letter, but I can't read the thing." I didn't have time for this today.

The letter was yellowed, looked like it had been around for a long time. I handed it back to her. "You read it to me. In English."

The look she gave me made my heart feel like it crawled right up into my throat. Everything was so serious with this girl.

She said, "*Oma* sent me a box last week. She sent shillings and a note. She said I should have this letter. She kept it for a long time because she wanted Mama's words with her."

I said, "You want to sit down? You're not looking so good."

Nicolette nodded and sat on the bed.

"Well go on then. I'm listening."

89

Dear Mother,   *12 April 1945*

How many years has it been since we've seen one another, seven now?

The loyalty you and Father have to Hitler is greater than your loyalty to your own blood, at least mine. You should know that I gave birth to a daughter three days ago. She is quite small, truly a miracle for us. Josef named her Nicolette, telling me her name means freedom of the people.

I hope someday you will meet her.

The war, Josef assures me, will end soon. He says the Red Army and the Americans are close to our borders. We pray that they arrive and release us from the blackness of this war. Josef promised me that when the war is over, we will borrow an automobile and drive to the town of Rust with Nicolette. It's next to a lake full of reeds. He tells me that a group of large white birds with black-tipped wings fly back to their nests in chimneys every Spring. They mate for life.

I hope you will come to visit us and meet Nicolette when the war ends.

I pray for you, Mother, every day.

Your daughter, with all my love,

Paulina

Not sure what I was supposed to say about it, I said, "That's a nice letter."

Nicolette looked at me with something I couldn't explain in her eyes.

She said, "You keep the baby."

"What do you mean," I said, "*keep* the baby?"

She said, "I cannot take a baby back with me to Vienna. My father will not—"

"—You just upset now. Your dad will be fine. It'll just take time. You ain't the first young woman to have a baby without getting married. Tell him it happens all the time here in America."

Nicolette stared at the floor. "I cannot—"

I don't know what happened in that flash of a second, but my words came out of me real fast. "Now let me tell you something here. You don't just *give* your baby away to someone like that. You hear me? This is a child. *Your* child."

Nicolette, sitting on the bed, looked like she was afraid of me.

But I felt something now going full force in my body and more words came rushing out. "And aren't you forgetting somethin'?" I said. "Look at me!"

Now there was definite fear on her face and she looked like she was going to cry but that didn't stop me. I said, "Look at my skin! You been in this country long enough to know you don't give a white baby to a black woman! Now there ain't nothing more to talk about." I grabbed the bucket off of the floor and left the room. But as soon as I took a few steps down the hall, something made me go straight back into the room. I looked right at her.

91

This time I lowered my voice to steady myself and spoke real slow. "Me and Jimmy, that's all we wanted was to have a baby, you know, start a family. And then he got sent off to the war. There was nothing more in this world that I wanted than a child with that man. And now you just...just telling me to *take* yours. What is wrong with you, child?"

Nicolette said, "I cannot take the baby to Vienna and I cannot stay here."

Lord, have mercy, I felt like grabbing that girl. Did she not hear a word I just said? I shook my head and walked out of that room.

~~~

In late February a woman hired me to play the violin at her father's funeral Mass. The family wanted only instrumental songs, no vocals. It was the morning of the day you were born. The church, pressed between two high-rise buildings on Madison Street, had three arched entrances; a stone crucifix hung above the center one. Two Franciscan brothers in brown robes and sandals greeted me inside. We walked past the mourners who spoke in murmured voices. They led me down the marble aisle to the side of the altar. Before a statue of Mary, I prepared my violin.

When the priest nodded from the back of the church, I lifted the violin to my shoulder. I felt weak and was unsure if I could play. My fingers released the first notes of Chopin's *Funeral March*, and an image of Alma and the women in her orchestra came to me. I continued. The pallbearers lifted the casket and walked down the aisle. As they lowered the casket before the altar, the priest swung a silver censer over the woman's deceased father, releasing its incense.

In the hospital room, the nurses heard my accent but did not ask where I was from. I told them I was from across the ocean, far from Chicago. I told them more than they wanted to know.

93

One nurse was pleasant to me; the other, the one with hair the color of old snow, spoke to me in short sentences. I asked her for a soft-boiled egg and a cut of sausage. She said I was not allowed to eat.

I traced the flowers on the hospital gown with my finger. They were like the tulips I drew when I was a young child. Mama watched me draw them on a large piece of paper with a letter U and a king's crown on top, a thin green stem with one leaf. Red, orange, yellow, blue, violet—the colors of the rainbow. Papa discovered my red tulips in one of his music books and slapped my hand. When I cried, he picked me up and held me until my tears stopped.

A nursing aide with long, straight hair walked into the room holding a Styrofoam cup. I wanted to tell her I did not want crushed ice. I wanted food from my country. I wanted Mama's t*afelspitz,* or Fraulein Elstein's *knodel.* But the stringy-haired girl did not bring me what I wanted.

I asked her where Tillie was.

The pain began to coil and strike within me and I clutched the bed rail. When Tillie walked into the room and saw me, she called for a nurse.

Soon my pain turned into soft colors.

The nurses did not want me to see you. But your bones were made of my bones. Your blood was mine.

The married couple waited for you in the waiting room. They lived in a large brick house in the far western suburbs. Months before, the social worker told us they had a bedroom painted pale pink like

swirls of cotton candy and a yard full of green grass
with an oak tree with a swing tied to its branch.

I wanted to name you Alma Joan.

Forgive me.

~~~

My grandmother used to tell me that you can't dwell on things you can't change. You have to keep moving in life, no matter what happens, or what life takes from you. So the morning Nicolette was to leave, I got myself out of bed and got dressed.

We rode the L to the airport in silence. Nicolette had only one suitcase and her violin case. When I seen planes fly overhead, I nudged her and said, "I think I'll get me one of those passports. Think your dad be okay with that? You know, a visit from me?"

Nicolette was holding herself in so tight I didn't think she'd answer me. She didn't turn her head but softly said, "Yes."

"Blanche will know where to get a passport," I said. "She'll go with me."

I tapped on her violin case. "You gonna keep playing, aren't you?"

Nicolette nodded.

I said, "You're really good. You know that?"

"Yes," she said. "I know."

I wasn't expecting no comment like that and it made me laugh out loud. "Well, all right then. Good. Glad we got that settled."

When the L stopped, we got off and started walking into the corridor of the airport. It was cold from all that wind blowing outside. Nicolette was looking all nervous, like she did when I first met her in my apartment.

There was no reason to make this any longer so I hugged her and said, "Promise you'll take good care of yourself. You hear me?"

"Yes," she said, not letting go. "I hear you."

"You coming back?"

Nicolette didn't answer me. We pulled apart and I handed her a package of Starburst. My eyes were stinging, but there was no way I was going to lose it standing there in that cold corridor. Nicolette walked away and then stopped and looked back at me. For a second, I thought the girl was going to run back to me. I waved her on.

Dear Lord, help me.

You will never know the truth, my child.

You will never know about your grandfather whose hand was shot when he refused to play the violin for Hitler's orchestra, or how the Russians were chased from my country with the Holy Rosary. You will never know about a girl who had to learn to forgive herself for taking confections from a soldier, or the woman who cared for your mother in America.

Sometimes, all we have to offer is love.

Nothing more.

About the Author

Shelly Drancik earned her MFA in fiction from Queens University of Charlotte. Her short fiction has appeared in various literary journals. The screenplay she adapted from this novella has earned numerous awards. Shelly lives in Chicago with her children.

About the Press

Unsolicited Press is a small publisher in Portland, Oregon. The press seeks to produce art, not commodity, from emerging and award-winning authors. Dedicated toward equality in publishing, Unsolicited Press publishes an equal number of men and women each year. Learn more at unsolicitedpress.com and connect with the press on Twitter and Instagram (@unsolicitedpress).